Thomas' Milkshake Muddle

• Three THOMAS & FRIENDS Stories •

Book & CD Edition

Random House 🏠 **New York**

A Random House PICTUREBACK® Book

Photographs by Terry Palone and Terry Permane

Thomas the Tank Engine & Friends™

CREATED BY BRITT ALLCROFT

Based on The Railway Series by The Reverend W Awdry.
© 2007 Gullane (Thomas) LLC. Thomas the Tank Engine & Friends and Thomas & Friends
are trademarks of Gullane (Thomas) LLC.
Thomas the Tank Engine & Friends & Design is Reg. U.S. Pat. & Tm. Off.
All rights reserved. Published in the United States by Random House Children's Books, a division of Random House, Inc.,
1745 Broadway, New York, NY 10019, and in Canada by Random House of Canada Limited, Toronto. PICTUREBACK, RANDOM
HOUSE and colophon, PLEASE READ TO ME and colophon, and LISTEN WITH ME BOOK & CD and design are registered trademarks of
Random House, Inc.
www.randomhouse.com/kids/thomas
www.thomasandfriends.com
Library of Congress Control Number: 2006937777   ISBN: 978-0-375-84227-6
MANUFACTURED IN CHINA   10 9 8 7 6 5 4 3 2 1

HiT entertainment

·Thomas' Milkshake Muddle·

Once a year, the children of Sodor are all invited to a special summer party. There was to be ice cream and cake for everyone.

Every engine wanted to be the one to take the children to the party. On the day of the party, Sir Topham Hatt came to Tidmouth Sheds.

Thomas hoped that *he* would be taking the children, but Sir Topham Hatt chose Emily.

He had other jobs for Thomas.

"Thomas, first you are to go to the Dairy to collect milk to make the ice cream. Then you must go to the farm on the other side of the Island to collect butter for cakes. All in time for the children's party."

Thomas set off proudly.

When Thomas arrived at the Dairy, the Manager told him he was to take the milk churns to the Ice Cream Factory. "You have to go *very* slowly," he told Thomas.

So Thomas steamed carefully away.

When Thomas stopped at a signal, he met Emily.

"Hello, slow coach!" she whistled.

"I'm not being a slow coach!" huffed Thomas. "I'm being reliable!"

"If you weren't a slow coach," Emily sniffed, "Sir Topham Hatt would have given you my job! I'm fast and I'm reliable. That's why I'm taking the children!"

Emily looked very pleased with herself.

This made Thomas cross. "I can be as fast as you!" he huffed.

"I'll race you to the next signal!" Emily whistled. And she steamed quickly away.

Thomas *wheesh*ed after her as fast as his pistons would pump! As he raced along, the milk churns rattled and rocked. . . .

They biffed and bashed. . . .

And at the next signal, Thomas raced ahead of Emily.

Thomas was very pleased.

He steamed off for the Ice Cream Factory, but he had completely forgotten about going slowly.

The Ice Cream Factory Manager was very happy. Thomas had delivered the milk in record time! Now the factory could make the ice cream for the party.

But when the Manager looked into one of the churns, he was very surprised.

"This milk is almost butter!" exclaimed the Manager.

The Factory Manager asked Thomas if the churns had rattled around. Thomas looked worried. "If you shake milk for long enough, it turns to butter," he told Thomas.

Thomas was very upset.

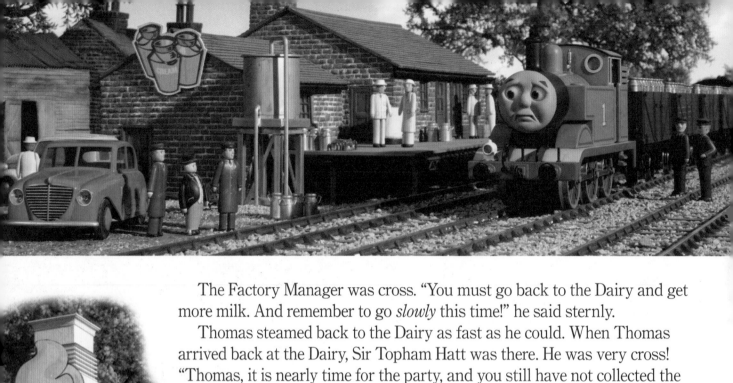

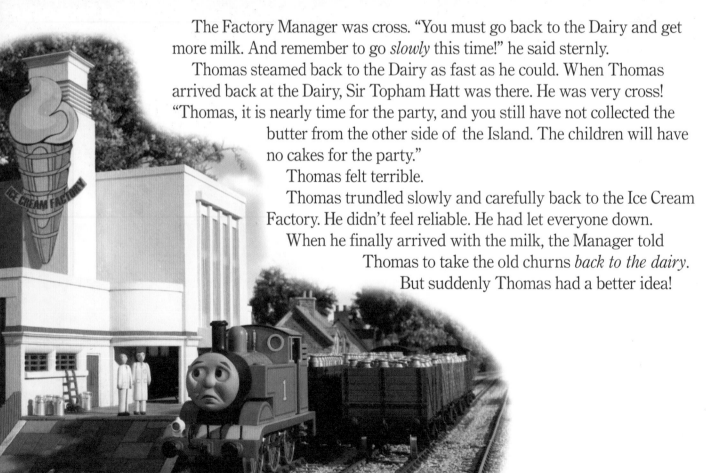

The Factory Manager was cross. "You must go back to the Dairy and get more milk. And remember to go *slowly* this time!" he said sternly.

Thomas steamed back to the Dairy as fast as he could. When Thomas arrived back at the Dairy, Sir Topham Hatt was there. He was very cross! "Thomas, it is nearly time for the party, and you still have not collected the butter from the other side of the Island. The children will have no cakes for the party."

Thomas felt terrible.

Thomas trundled slowly and carefully back to the Ice Cream Factory. He didn't feel reliable. He had let everyone down.

When he finally arrived with the milk, the Manager told Thomas to take the old churns *back to the dairy*.

But suddenly Thomas had a better idea!

Thomas steamed along with the milk churns even faster than he had before. He huffed up Gordon's Hill . . . and chuffed down to the Valley. He raced like a rocket . . . and he *wheesh*ed like the wind.

The churns in Thomas' freight cars rattled and rolled . . . they clanked and crashed . . . and biffed and bashed. Even the cows and sheep looked up to see what the noise was. But Thomas couldn't stop until he got to the bakery!

As he arrived, he blew his whistle long and hard.
"I need butter, not milk!" cried the Baker. He was
surprised to see the milk churns.
"Look inside the churns!" tooted Thomas.

The Baker couldn't believe his eyes! The "almost-butter" was now butter! Enough to make *all* the cakes for the party!

Sir Topham Hatt had heard what Thomas had done. He came to see him.

Thomas thought Sir Topham Hatt would be cross. He was very worried.

But Sir Topham Hatt smiled. "Thomas, you have saved the children's party!" he boomed. "So today, that makes you the most reliable engine on the whole of Sodor!"

And later, Thomas had his most important job yet—as Guest of Honor at the children's party! There was lots of ice cream and plenty of cakes. Everyone had a wonderful time. The children cheered for Thomas.

Thomas felt very proud.

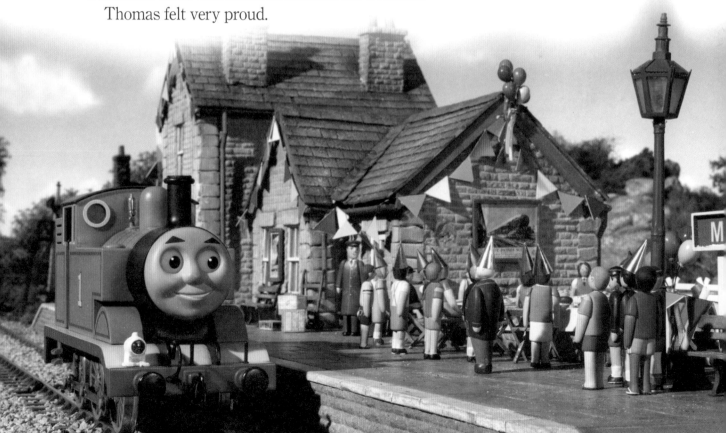

•Toby Feels Left Out•

It was springtime on the Island of Sodor. All the engines were working hard in the sunshine.

One morning, Sir Topham Hatt arrived at Tidmouth Sheds. He had some exciting news. "The new Sodor Museum opens soon," he announced. "Lots of very important people will be coming to the Island for the Grand Opening."

"What's a museum?" asked Percy.

"It's a place where they put *old* things so people can stand and look at them," huffed Gordon.

"I want you all to look your best, so everyone is to have a repaint."

All the engines were very pleased.

Later that morning, Toby met James at Knapford Station. "Have you heard about the opening of the new museum?" puffed James. "We're all having a repaint. I shall look wonderful with a brand-new coat of red paint."

"I've not heard about that," said Toby. "Why hasn't Sir Topham Hatt told me?"

"You must have been left out," chuffed James, and he steamed away.

That night, Toby couldn't sleep. He kept worrying about what James had said. "Why hasn't Sir Topham Hatt told me about the museum?" he wondered. "Why have I been left out?"

By the next morning, Toby thought he knew the answer. He met Thomas at Abbey Station.

"Have *you* heard about the museum?" asked Toby.

"Yes," puffed Thomas excitedly. "We're all being repainted!"

"I'm not," puffed Toby sadly. "But I think I know why. I am a very old steam tram. Maybe Sir Topham Hatt has decided to put me inside the museum."

Thomas wasn't so sure. "Why don't you ask him?" huffed Thomas helpfully.

Toby looked worried. He was frightened of what Sir Topham Hatt might say.

"Must go," puffed Thomas. "Really Useful Engines are really busy ones." And he chuffed away.

Toby thought for a moment. "I'll show Sir Topham Hatt that he can't put me in a museum," said Toby. "I'll show him *I'm* a Really Useful Engine."

Toby arrived at Tidmouth Sheds. Sir Topham Hatt was talking to Emily.
"Emily, you must go to the Yard for your repaint," said Sir Topham Hatt.
Emily was very happy.

"Another engine must collect your flour,"
said Sir Topham Hatt.

"I'll do it, Sir," said Toby quickly.

"Thank you," smiled Sir Topham Hatt. And before
he could say anything else, Toby steamed off. He
didn't want Sir Topham Hatt to tell him he was going
to be put in a museum.

Toby waited impatiently at the flour mill. "Hurry
up, hurry up," he *wheesh*ed. "I must get to the docks as
soon as I can."

When Toby delivered the flour, he saw Sir Topham Hatt standing on the dockside. He was talking to the Dock Master.

Sir Topham Hatt saw Toby. He wanted to speak to him, but Toby steamed off as fast as he could.

Later, Toby saw Thomas again. He was pulling Annie and Clarabel. "I'm off for my repaint," chuffed Thomas happily.

"I can pull Annie and Clarabel for you," said Toby.

"Thank you, Toby," tooted Thomas.

So Toby pulled Annie and Clarabel on Thomas' Branch Line.

And while James was getting a shiny new coat of red paint, Toby collected coal cars from the mine for James.

And while Percy was having *his* repaint, Toby shunted freight cars full of stone in the Quarry for Percy, even though it was dusty, dirty work.

At last, Toby had finished. He was very tired and very dirty.

Suddenly he saw Sir Topham Hatt waiting by the track. Toby still didn't want to speak to Sir Topham Hatt. Quickly he reversed into a siding and didn't see that a big rock had fallen on the line.

"Bust my cowcatchers!" he cried.

Luckily, no one was hurt. But Toby's axle and his cowcatchers were broken. He couldn't move!

Sir Topham Hatt hurried over. "Why have you been running away from me all day?" he asked.

"I—I don't want to be put in a museum," Toby said sadly.

"Why would I do *that,* Toby?" asked Sir Topham Hatt.

"Because a museum is full of old things and I'm an old steam tram. And I'm not Really Useful anymore."

Sir Topham Hatt smiled. "Toby, you may be old, but you are far too useful to be put in the museum. You have worked harder today than any other engine. And as Sodor's only steam tram, I have a very special job for you. First you will have a special polish. Then you are to take all the visitors to the museum for the Grand Opening."

Toby felt very happy. He let out a great *wheesh* of steam!

"I've been trying to tell you that all day," added Sir Topham Hatt.

Toby smiled. He felt very silly.

So Toby's axle and cowcatchers were repaired, and then he was polished until he looked as good as new.

On the day of the museum opening, Toby picked up the visitors at the Docks and puffed them proudly to the new museum.

Toby was proud to be old. And he was even prouder to be the only Really Useful Steam Tram on the Island of Sodor!

•Thomas and the New Engine•

The trains on the Island of Sodor keep very busy. There are always lots of jobs to do.

One morning, Sir Topham Hatt came to Tidmouth Sheds. "A new engine has arrived on the Island," he announced. "His name is Neville. You must all make him feel welcome. A happy engine is a Useful Engine."

Later, Thomas was stopped at a signal. The Signalman called down to Thomas. "The bridge ahead is unsafe. Thomas, you are to collect a piece of ironwork so the bridge can be repaired."

"Yes, sir," huffed Thomas.

At the yards, 'Arry and Bert were with Neville, the new engine. Neville was a steamie, but he had a square body like a diesel. Neville was backing up towards some trucks.

"Nearly there," said 'Arry cheekily.

"Nearly there," said Bert naughtily.

Then there was trouble!

"Watch where you're going, clumsy wheels!" 'Arry and Bert laughed.

Neville looked sad.

"It's not our fault if you're a silly steamie!" oiled Bert. And they laughed even harder.

Thomas arrived at the yards. He could see 'Arry and Bert laughing with Neville. "That must be the new engine," he thought. "He must be friends with the diesels."

Thomas arrived at Knapford Station.

"Have you seen the new engine yet?" asked James.

"Yes," said Thomas. "But we'd better be careful. I saw him at the yards with 'Arry and Bert. They were laughing together."

James was shocked! A steamie friendly with diesels?!?

As Thomas left, Edward pulled in.

"Have you heard about the new engine?" snorted James . . . and he started to tell Edward all about Neville.

Later, Edward was taking on water. He was talking to Percy. "That new steamie, Neville, is best friends with the diesels," Edward puffed. "He doesn't want to be with steamies at all."

"How do you know?" peeped Percy.

"James told me, and Thomas told him!" whistled Edward.

Later, Percy met Emily at a red signal. "Don't go near Neville, the new engine," he told her. "The diesels have told him to biff into steamies. Edward told me—James told Edward—and they heard all about it from Thomas!"

When Thomas arrived at Abbey Station, Sir Topham Hatt was there. "Thomas, you must warn all engines not to cross the bridge until it's repaired," he boomed.

Thomas felt proud. It was a *very* useful job. Just then, he heard a whistle. Someone was coming! Thomas had to warn them. It was Neville . . . pulling *Annie and Clarabel*! Thomas was shocked! Annie and Clarabel were *his* carriages!

"Hello!" puffed Neville cheerfully.

"I'm not talking to you!" Thomas huffed crossly.

Neville didn't know what he had done.

Then Emily pulled in next to Neville. "Hello," said Neville happily.

Emily let out a *wheesh* of steam. "It's no use trying to make friends with me. I know you're going to biff into all the steamies! Just like 'Arry and Bert told you to!"

Thomas was surprised. But the Station Master blew his whistle. And Neville puffed sadly away.

"Where did you hear that Neville is going to biff into all the steamies?" Thomas asked Emily.

"Don't you know?" Emily whistled. "Percy told me, Edward told Percy, James told Edward, and *you* told James!" huffed Emily.

"But I only said to James that I'd seen Neville with 'Arry and Bert. . . ."

Then Toby arrived. "Have you heard about Neville, the new engine?" he puffed. "Henry saw 'Arry and Bert be horrible to him at the yards!"

Emily was shocked. Thomas couldn't believe it! Neville wasn't friends with the diesels after all!

"Where was Neville going?" Emily tooted.

"Cinders and ashes!" cried Thomas. "Neville's heading for the broken bridge! I must stop him!"

Neville was speeding through the countryside as fast as he could.

Suddenly Neville saw a barrier on the track. He slammed on his brakes, but it was too late....

Neville was in terrible trouble! He was on the broken end of the bridge!

Thomas knew it was all his fault! Suddenly he had an idea! Thomas steamed slowly and carefully onto the bridge. He gently bumped Clarabel and was coupled up. Thomas was very scared. Slowly and steadily, he began to pull Neville back from the edge. The bridge made a creaking noise. Thomas knew he must hurry! He pulled as hard as he could. . . .

And with one big puff, he pulled Neville's wheels off the bridge! Thomas had done it! He had saved Neville and Annie and Clarabel!

"Thank you," whistled Neville.

"I should have warned you," puffed Thomas. "But I was too busy believing silly stories. I thought you didn't like steamies. But now I know I was wrong."

Thomas gave Neville a long, friendly *toot toot*.

Neville was very happy. At last, he knew he had a good friend in Thomas.